The Basket Maker and the Spinner

Other Walker Books by Beatrice Siegel

Indians of the Woodland
A New Look at the Pilgrims
Fur Trappers and Traders
The Steam Engine
The Sewing Machine

Beatrice Siegel

The Basket Maker
and the Spinner

Illustrated by William Sauts Bock

Walker and Company
New York

First published in the United States of America in 1987 by the Walker Publishing Company, Inc.

Published simultaneously in Canada by John Wiley & Sons Canada, Limited, Rexdale, Ontario

Library of Congress Cataloging-in-Publication Data

Siegel, Beatrice.
  The basket maker and the spinner.

  Summary: Tells the stories of the Indian basket weavers and colonial spinners of early America and discusses the preservation of their craft in a time of advanced technology.
  Bibliography: p.
  1. Indians—Basket making—Juvenile literature.
2. Basket makers—Juvenile literature. 3. Spinning—
Juvenile literature. [1. Indians of North America—
Basket making. 2. Basket making. 3. Spinning.
4. United States—Social life and customs—Colonial
period, ca. 1600–1775. 5. Handicraft] I. Bock,
William Sauts, 1939–   ill. II. Title.
E59.B3S56 1987   746.41'2'08997   86-32617
ISBN 0-8027-6694-3
      0-8027-6695-1 (Reinforced)

Printed in the United States of America

10 9 8 7 6 5 4 3 2 1

To my daughter Andra
and my granddaughter Julia
carrying on
the artists' gifts today.

Contents

Contents

Introduction

"Atisket atasket,
A green and yellow basket:
I wrote a letter to my love
And on the way I lost it.
I lost it, I lost it,
And on the way I lost it."

In the headlong rush to the modern world, we lost more than the letter. We also lost the basket, for modern technology has all but swallowed up the great art of basketry of our Indian ancestors.

If you can work a computer, do you care about baskets? If you can land on the moon, or if you can retrieve treasure buried in deep seas over hundreds of years, where does the basket fit in?

Still, like old memories, baskets linger on, and we like to look back to an earlier time, to the way the first people in this country lived.

Thinking of baskets for even a few minutes makes us pause in the heady race of today's world. We escape from the world's problems: problems of crime, drugs, pollution, and nuclear missiles. Baskets speak of a quieter, softer time, of communal caring, of patience and perseverance. Baskets bring back to us the inner solitude and artistry of Indian women whose role in thousands of years of the continent's history we have yet to appreciate.

The spinner also talks of an earlier time but in a different voice. Spinners were not native to this soil. They were the colonists who introduced European ideas and technology to the eastern seaboard.

Though the basket maker and the spinner had much in common, they told different stories.

The Leaves Are Falling

The sunflowers stood tall and stately. They lingered in the garden like the last rays of summer sun. Yawata, looking over the land in the early fall, knew that the sunflower heads would soon tilt downward, drooping like a sleepy child. The nights were cooler, the days shorter, and the russet autumn leaves were falling. Sometimes the world stood still, but now all around her was movement. Flocks of ducks and geese, in flight to warm climates, filled the marshes. Often the sun itself was blocked out by thousands of birds migrating south.

Yawata also moved to the beat and rhythm of the world around her. She was a woman of one of the largest New England tribes, called the Wampanoag, and had been born and reared in the New England woodlands where native people had lived for ten thousand years. She was brought up from infancy to feel at one with her surroundings, to listen to the murmuring winds in the woods. Her strong straight body moved easily in soft leather clothes. A headband held

back her long straight hair. Under her feet, shod in soft deer skin *mocussinass* (moccasins), she felt the contour of every stone and the shape of the earth. Overhead the color of the morning sky announced the weather. Trees and plants gave her messages of the changing seasons.

Yawata's religion strengthened her ties to nature. She and her people had deep faith in supernatural forces and in the belief that spirits resided everywhere in nature: in animals, in plants, and in people. Spirits could be reached through an intermediary known as a *shaman,* or medicine man, a person of strong supernatural powers. Through special rituals and ceremonies, the shaman could call on the rain spirit to end a drought, or on the spirit that protected hunters; he took care of the sick, or kept a watchful eye on children, or guarded warriors during a war. Over these many individual spirits reigned the Great Spirit, known to the Wampanoag as *Manitou.* The whole living world was thus linked together, and every aspect of nature had deep religious significance.

Now that the leaves were falling, Yawata knew that she would have to dismantle her summer home. Her wigwam, like the others in the village, stood on cleared ground around the communal center. In back of the homes stretched acres of farm land.

In all the years of their long history, Yawata's people had moved from season to season to be near food. For the winter she would seek the safety of a warm, sheltered valley where men would hunt deer and other animals. They would also help build strong winter homes to withstand snow and sleet. Summer or winter, wigwams looked as if they grew out of the earth. They were made of saplings dug into the ground, arched over, and lashed together. Over the frame, women placed tree bark or tightly woven cattail mats that repelled rain. Indoors, mats were used for flooring, wall covering, beds, and seats. Loosely woven summer mats were often left behind with other household items too heavy to carry.

Though Yawata worked from morning to night she did not complain but accepted her role in the village and tribe. Her three children were now learning traditional patterns of work in which each one contributed to the welfare of the whole community.

This life style also made it easier for Yawata to get through the endless round of chores. She never worked alone, but in a group of women. Together they built homes and cared for them, raised the children, gathered and prepared the food, tanned skins, and cut and sewed them into clothing. They carried water and wood. They worked on clay for pottery and spent every available moment weaving baskets and mats for their practical needs. Perhaps more important than most of their chores was their work as farmers. Yawata's children, as well as other village children, helped their mothers in the planting, weeding, and harvesting of crops. Yawata's youngest daughter, six-year-old Quenimiquet, had a special task. She and other youngsters sat among the crops many hours each day to shoo away the birds.

Yawata's husband, a warrior and hunter, worked alongside other village men building canoes and making tools. They spent long hours shaping bone and stone into chisels, hoes, and knives.

The village center was the meeting place for women, men, and children. Here they relaxed and enjoyed themselves in athletic games and, sometimes, at gam-

bling. The center was also the gathering place for religious ceremonies and dances.

Over the years village women grew more kinds of vegetables and harvested bigger crops. Sometimes they produced more food than the men did in winter hunting. Maybe someday women would grow enough farm produce so that they could, if they wished, live in one place. Then Yawata would be able to live year-round in her village, near her vegetable farm and the sunflowers.

Though it was now fall, Yawata paused in her round of work to think back for a few minutes to early spring, to the month of March, when the sap flowed in trees and spawning fish filled the rivers. That was when her whole village camped in the woods near the maple trees to tap them and make sweet syrup.

Then came *Sequanankeeswush* (late April and early May), the month "when they set Indian corn." The land had long ago been cleared for farming. Into small mounds of earth women placed both corn and bean seeds. Between the mounds, they planted squash, pumpkin, and peas. This year Yawata planted sunflowers, while others planted Jerusalem artichokes. By harvest time, the garden plots were a tangle of greenery. Bean vines were curled around corn stalks for support while pumpkin vines crept along the ground. But the women and children who cared for the crops every single day knew exactly what was going on. They carefully weeded, removed harmful insects, and shooed away animals and birds.

Maize, or corn, the staple crop, had multicolored kernels of white, red, blue, and yellow. Starting in August, the first ears of corn were picked and placed on mats to dry in the sun. At night, women covered

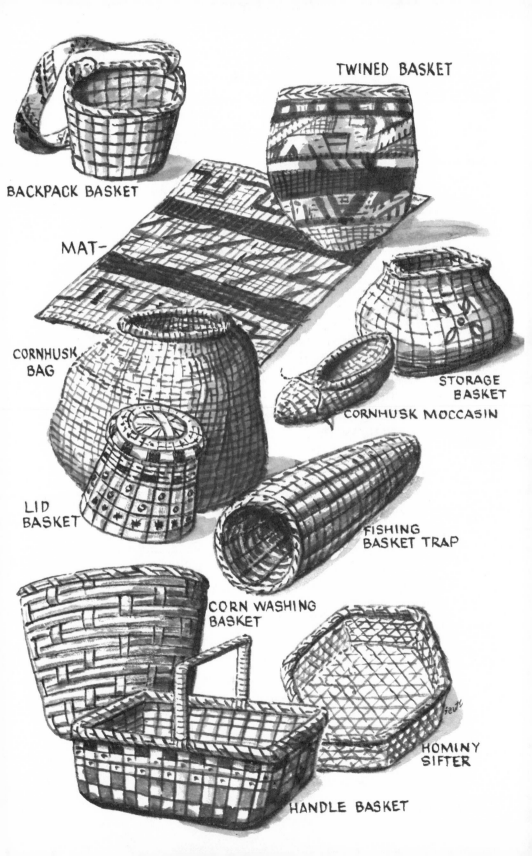

BACKPACK BASKET

TWINED BASKET

MAT

CORNHUSK BAG

STORAGE BASKET

CORNHUSK MOCCASIN

LID BASKET

FISHING BASKET TRAP

CORN WASHING BASKET

HOMINY SIFTER

HANDLE BASKET

the corn with more mats for protection against both dampness and hungry animals. When dried, the corn was placed in large baskets and hung on walls of the home to be eaten whole or beaten into flour for pancakes and bread.

Hanging on the wall in other baskets were dried nuts and berries picked during the summer.

Yawata and other village women were in charge of the home and the food supply. They regulated how much corn could be eaten and how much had to be stored over the winter until the next spring. When families returned to summer lodgings, and until the first harvest in August, they lived on fish, wild berries and nuts, and the food carefully stored in deep baskets in underground pits. These deep holes in the earth were padded with mats to keep the damp earth away from the baskets of food. Additional mats were wrapped around the baskets themselves to protect them from rain and foraging animals.

Mats and baskets! They were used for everything. For storage; for pots, pans, and dishes; for bags and boxes. There were baskets for trapping, fishing, and hunting; for cradles; for carrying water; and for cooking. They came in all sizes and shapes: giant sized or tiny, round or square, with handles or not, covered or not, flat or deep, soft in texture or stiff and firm.

Stored in Yawata's home were wild grasses, cattails, twigs, and strips of bark ready to be woven into baskets. But Yawata was not unique. The world of basketry belonged to women along with all their other work. Going back thousands of years and in every part of the continent women were the basket makers.

Baskets Everywhere

Not only in the Northeast where Yawata lived but in every part of the country, women made baskets. It was a craft dating back thousands of years to ancient times, when women tried to ease their household work. They became inventive, and made practical products out of the raw materials they found in nature.

They pulled together tall grasses and twigs and interlaced them. To carry babies, they wove material into backpacks and cradles. To transport water, they made water buckets. To prepare and serve food, they made cooking vessels, containers, and dishes. And just as women were able to find edible berries, roots, and nuts, so were they adept at gathering grasses, plant stems, leaves, or whatever was handy, for the weaving process.

Everywhere women found material for basketry. No region escaped their searching eyes, whether they lived in mountain cliffs, canyon valleys, or on fertile plains; whether they were nomads wandering from place to

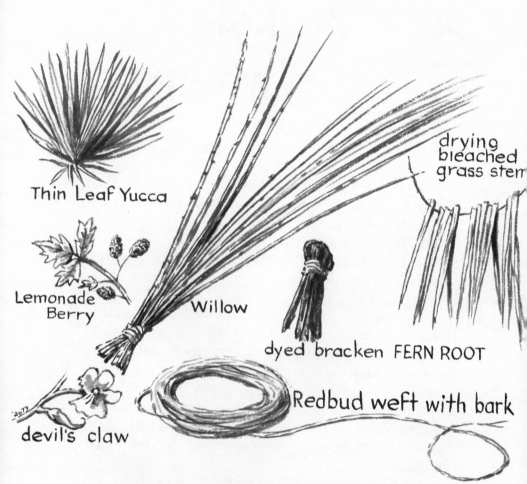

Thin Leaf Yucca

Lemonade Berry

Willow

devil's claw

dyed bracken FERN ROOT

drying bleached grass stem

Redbud weft with bark

BASKET WEAVING MATERIALS

place or were settled near lakes and rivers. Even the desert yielded its scrubby plants, the prickly pear and mesquite.

Women learned from experience the best season to collect material. They gathered what they needed and bundled it to be worked on when they had time. They also devised processes for transforming tough fibers into flexible strands. It was hard, tedious work, but they persevered.

Their strong hands were their best tools, but women also used their teeth to crack away the woody coverings over inner fibers. Or they softened tough twigs by steaming or soaking them in hot water. Some women buried twigs in damp earth for several days to make them pliant. The most common tools were stone or bone knives and awls. They used knives to cut and shape grasses and twigs. The awl, a pointed instrument, was used in the weaving process to punch holes for the interlacing of different strands of material.

For many women it was not enough to turn out only functional objects. They created beautiful baskets, ones in which they expressed their feelings and thoughts. In doing so, basketry was both a practical craft and an artistic expression. They devised many ways to do this by varying both structure and design.

Women wove designs into baskets with different widths and textured fibers. Or they made dyes from plants, tree bark, and berries, and interwove red, blue, yellow, or black strands. They created geometric patterns or deftly wove images of birds, flowers, and animals. Some ornamented baskets with dyed quills, feathers, leather fringe, or shell beads.

No school taught these skills. Nor were techniques and patterns written up in books or pinned on walls.

The skill, springing from necessity, was stowed in the collective memories of the people and taught by mothers to daughters over thousands of years.

The craft was not studied only by a few but learned by women generally and practiced communally. It was a household industry. Wherever women gathered together they would pick up their basket work, indoors in rain or snow, outdoors in the sun; while they watched children, talked to friends, or cooked over the fire. It was part of the day's work, for baskets were fragile, easily damaged, and had to be replaced.

bone knife

stone knife

bone awl

splitting willow with teeth and hands

tools for basket weaving

PIMA BASKET MAKERS

For the very gifted, basketry was a special art. These women searched for rare materials and worked out new techniques and patterns.

When working, most women sat on the ground with feet tucked in underneath, the basket on their laps. A few sat with feet stretched out in front. Others were comfortable in a kneeling position. Some even sat with their knees raised under their chins, their hands circling their knees, free to do basketry. That was the preferred position of the Tlingit women of southern Alaska who were among the great basket makers. The Tlingit made baskets out of spruce roots. Their Aleut neighbors used shredded grasses.

BASKETS

Aleut

Tlingit

Pomo Feather

Other great basket makers lived in southern Arizona where the Pima created geometric patterns out of local plants like tisal willow, squaw weed, and devil's claw. In northern Arizona, the Hopi made colorful designs out of sumac twigs, yucca, and willow. The Pomo along the Pacific coast made extraordinary baskets decorated with feathers. And even in the barren lands of Death Valley, women found material to create finely woven products, while the bold and adventurous Apache used basketry to express their dynamic spirit.

What started out as a simple method of webbing or interweaving a few twigs and grasses developed over thousands of years into sophisticated and varied skills. A popular basket technique was *coiling,* a continuous pattern in which leaves or splints were wound or coiled around other material which might be grass or wood rods. There was also *twining,* in which two or more horizontal elements were twisted around rigid vertical material. Basic techniques had many variations that gave novelty to the finished products.

By using the specific materials at hand, the people of each region of the country became known for their unique style of basketry.

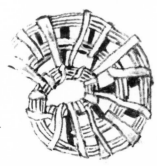

COILING

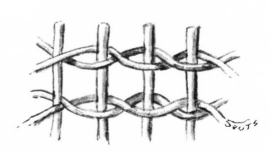

TWINING

"The White Man's Ship"

Special to the Northeast and to the New England region where Yawata lived was the use of tree bark to make practical articles. These items were often put together quickly for immediate use and then discarded. They came in handy at sugaring time when families needed containers to collect sap.

"Barking" was done in the spring when villagers camped out to tap the maple trees. The preferred tree was white birch, though usable bark also came from the elm, chestnut, oak, fir, and cedar.

In a traditional technique, a standing tree was encircled with two cuts ranging in width from a few inches to three or four feet. A third cut ran up the tree trunk to connect the other two. Sometimes a tall tree was cut down. Then using strong sticks or chisel-shaped tools, men and women pried the bark from the tree trunk. To make the heavy outer bark more pliable, it was beaten with a woodheaded hammer called a maul. Other bark was softened by soaking in hot water. Out of now pliant bark, Yawata and other women made not only

TREE BARKING

buckets for maple syrup but also cradles, utensils, cups, and even pots that could be hung over steaming stones and used for cooking.

The bark was folded over into a required object and stitched together with split spruce or cedar roots, though the hemp plant provided the strongest thread. Women twisted hemp fibers on their bare thighs to make them thin and strong.

Early European explorers and traders, who had been making incursions into the region for many years, commented on the variety of woven and bark articles they found. The English missionary Daniel Gookin wrote (years later) about his surprise at finding baskets made of "maise husks, others of a kind of silk grass, others of a kind of wild hemp, and some of bark of trees. Many of these are very neat . . . with the portraitures of birds, beasts, fishes, and flowers upon them in color."

To ornament her baskets and bark objects, Yawata used berries for dyes. She also made other colors from minerals in the soil. Graphite gave her the color black; ocher produced red and yellow.

Yellow! Yawata looked again at the sunflowers. She had to gather the yellow sun petals for a dye. She would also use the sunflower stems in basketry even though the fibers were so fine that they did not show. But like corn husks, they were soft and provided a natural color. She looked at the rushes she had gathered in August and at the sweet grasses drying.

The sunflowers alone would keep her busy all fall. The disk of seeds, or achenes, would soon be ripe for picking. They were tightly packed against each other as if placed there by hand. She served the seeds as they were, to be cracked open and eaten; or she stored

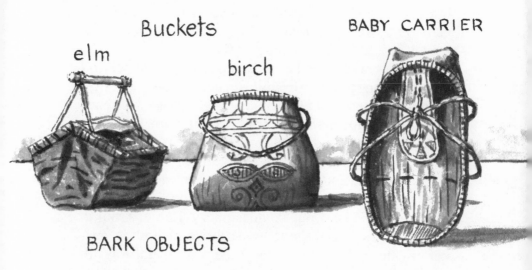

Buckets

elm

birch

BABY CARRIER

BARK OBJECTS

them. Often she beat them into a flour and paste for break and cakes.

Yawata had planted sunflowers not only because they were bright against the northern woods, but because every part of the plant was valuable. In themselves, the seeds were a food; the petals made a yellow dye; stalks were used in basketry. But above all, sunflower seeds made a precious oil when they were pounded into a mass and thrown into boiling water. At the point when oil floated on top of the kettle in large quantities, the water was cooled and the oil skimmed off. It was used as a food seasoning, a hair tonic, or as a base for the pigments that people painted on their faces for religious dances.

All around Yawata that autumn were familiar sights and sounds. Late corn was spread out in the sun to dry. Small animals were running through the ground

LADLE

CONTAINER for maple sap

TRAY

grass and up the trees, children scampering after them. But Yawata was uneasy as she thought about dismantling her summer home. And she knew why.

Kitonuck—"the white man's ship"—lay at anchor off the coast. It was another of many large wooden vessels with heavy canvas sails that had landed in recent months. On these boats came a strange people wearing strange clothes, speaking an unfamiliar language.

Yawata, like all the village people for miles around, knew about these strangers. She had seen them and also had heard about the explorers, traders, and sailors who had visited the villages. As a result of their visits, terrible things had happened. There had been violent skirmishes along the coast in which Indians had been kidnapped and a few sold into slavery. Worst of all was the spread of diseases common in Europe but

to which the native people had developed no immunity. Diseases such as smallpox, plague, and measles swept through the villages. In 1616 and 1617 a terrible epidemic ran rampant along the coast, devastating whole villages of people including the Wampanoag. It may have been the plague or typhoid, but the native population had no experience with such pestilence and were unable to treat it. Among the thousands who died were hunters and warriors, leaving the villagers unprotected. And now some of these same strange people who had caused so much havoc had arrived and settled on the land nearby. Who were they? Who were these families of men, women, and children so like her own family and yet so different?

Yawata had not paid much attention to the stories that had circulated through the villages for the past few years. Her people had taught the newcomers how to live in the woodlands and how to plant corn. They taught them how to fish, how to build homes, and how to keep warm over the cold winter. A white child, lost in the wilderness, had been found by Yawata's people and returned to the parents. Yawata herself had used a metal pot that the village women had gotten in exchange for baskets. It was strong and did not break.

According to Yawata's way of thinking, there was room for everyone to share the land in common, to use its plants and fruits. But events were not developing that way, in the way of her people. She was worried. Though everything still looked the same, there was a

sense of foreboding, of great changes taking place. She feared the unknown, a people whose spirit was so different from hers.

Sometimes Yawata had a nightmare thought that she would not be able to return to her village in the spring, to her vegetable garden and the sunflowers. The earth she stood on was vital to her, it connected her to the world and was the foundation of her life. If ever she was separated from it, she would be desolate.

The Spinner

Mary Allen was just plain Mary to her friends. She was a slim, dark-haired woman whose sleep was still disturbed by dreams of her village back in England. It was only a few years ago that she, her husband, and four children had joined hundreds of others on an old sailing vessel that took them across the ocean to a new world.

During the day she was too busy to dream or to think back to her native land. Like the Indian woman, Yawata, her days were filled with responsibilities that kept her busy from morning to night.

In many ways Mary's life was easier than Yawata's. She did not move around seasonally but lived in one place. And Mary had the use of metal and iron utensils, pots, and pans that did not have to be constantly replaced. She had brought over from England bedding, small pieces of furniture, farm implements, and tools. Despite advantages, Mary's workday never ended. She raised the children, prepared and served food. She hauled wood and water from outdoors, churned butter, dipped candles, made soap, and planted a vegetable garden. She helped her husband on the farm during harvest and put up vegetables and meat for the winter. And all year round, in every spare moment, she was busy at the spinning wheel or the loom.

On Sundays, Mary and her family filed down the path to the village church to worship a single God in the ways of their religion.

Unlike Yawata who worked in a group of women, Mary worked alone in her home. Only on Sundays at church, or at village socials, did she get to sit and talk with friends. But Mary had a different set of values than Yawata and the Indian people. Though she worked hard for many reasons, it was especially important to make a success of the farm and fields. They were private property belonging to Mary and her hus-

band. All the newcomers felt the way Mary Allen did. They had a sense of individualism—of private ownership and private possessions. They traveled across the ocean so that they could own and farm land. Many had the use of domesticated animals. The horse pulled the plow; the cows, chickens, and hogs provided food. The sheep were shorn for wool. And to keep their animals from wandering onto other people's private land, fences appeared on the woodland landscape.

Newcomers changed the land in other ways too. The sounds they brought with them ruptured woodland silence, a silence that had long ago absorbed the beat of drums. Now roaring through the forests were musket shot fired by militia out on daily practice. There was the crash of iron axes felling trees, the clatter of a scythe hitting rock. On Sundays church bells rang out.

Mary and her family were soon joined by hundreds

of others. They all wanted land and so took over the
fields that once belonged to Yawata and her people.
From the thatched-roof log cabin that Mary had at first
lived in, she and the family moved into a large clap-
board house. She now had a huge downstairs room
that spanned the whole floor, and above was the
sleeping loft. The best part of the house was the vast
fireplace that became the center of the household.
Hanging from hooks or from a pole were pots and
pans. On the mantle stood candlesticks. The floor was
a clutter of short-legged pots and trivets for cooking
food over a bed of coals. Along the wall stood tubs for

salting meat and tubs for milk maturing into cheese. Near the hearth stood the spinning wheel. Though Mary had brought some clothes with her, they were patched and repatched. Cargo ships carrying clothing rarely arrived. Either they sank during stormy ocean crossings, or they were plundered by pirates.

At first Mary and other families had tried to wear the same soft leather clothes as the Indians, but they were accustomed to the feel of cloth. By the late 1630s most homes had spinning wheels.

Mary, like her mother and grandmother, was an expert at the wheel. She had grown up with it and at age

eight had taken her place in the family as a spinner. Now she was teaching the skill to her eight year old, Bridget. The more hands that worked the wheel, keeping it busy all day long, the more yarn for fabric for dresses, shirts, and linens.

But before Mary or Bridget could make yarn, there was the long tedious process of preparing flax or wool for the wheel. The process involved the whole family.

Mary had already selected a patch of ground for flax seed, and in early May, planting time, she scattered the seeds over the field so that they were close together.

Weeding started when the plants were three to four inches high. This turned out to be a delicate procedure because the plant stalks were fragile. To avoid crushing them, Mary and the children walked among the plants barefooted.

Plants were pulled up sometime at the end of June or early July when the lower portion of the stem had turned yellow. By then the plant had produced its delicate blue flower.

The purpose of the processing was to get at the fibers within the woody stem. The first step was to spread the plants out in the sun to dry for a day or two. Then came *rippling*. The flax stalks were drawn through an iron wire comb to break off the seeds. Like the Indians, they used every part of the plant. The seeds were either fed to cattle or turned into oil.

The next step was *retting* or rotting, a process of soaking plant fibers until they were fermented and could be separated. After the fibers were separated, they were again cleaned and spread out in the sun to dry.

Then came the *flax-breaker* with its long bars and beater to break the fibers down further. To separate the rough and short fibers from the long ones, they were *hackled* or put through a block of metal teeth. They were continously cleaned, separated, soaked, and combed. At last they were as thin as hairs and ready for the spinning wheel.

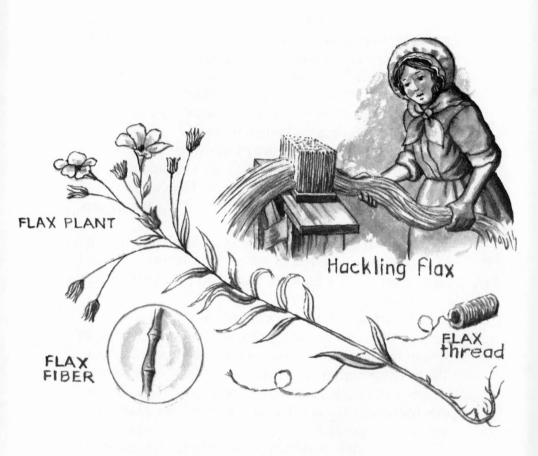

FLAX PLANT

Hackling Flax

FLAX FIBER

FLAX thread

Processing wool was much easier. Once a year, Mary watched her husband cut the rough curly wool from the sheep. Like flax, the wool was put through a process of cleaning, sorting, and combing or carding. Carding the wool by brushing it with combs that have strong metal teeth was easy but tiresome.

There was not time enough in the day or week for all the chores. At an early age, children did their share in the home and fields. At six years of age, they could be found bent over tables carding wool. In the average colonial family children did not have much time to play, and they were not educated at schools in reading and writing. Instead, they were educated at home in the practical matters of working on a farm, feeding cattle, and repairing tools.

Though Mary grabbed odd moments during the day to sit at the wheel, she really concentrated on spinning in the winter, from the month before Christmas until the spring planting season. From dawn to dusk the whir of the spinning wheel filled the home.

CARDING WOOL

The Distaff and the Spindle

The purpose of spinning was to draw out, twist, and wind a mass of fibers into one continuous strand of yarn. Whether it was flax or wool, it was piled or wrapped onto the distaff of the spinning wheel. This was the stick or staff set into the table of the wheel. By turning the wheel, by hand or foot treadle, the fibers were drawn out of the mass and spun onto the spindle, a short tapering stick notched at one end.

Like basketry, the art of spinning goes back thousands of years. And like basketry, spinning was women's work, practiced by queens in their palaces and by the poor in simple homes.

Spinning yarn and weaving cloth were so basic to the well-being of a country that the distaff became the honored symbol of women's work. Images of the distaff and the spindle adorn old parchment scrolls and sculptured stone dating back to ancient Egypt, Babylonia, and Greece. For thousands of years, women did their spinning by hand. They are portrayed holding the distaff in one hand and winding the thread onto the

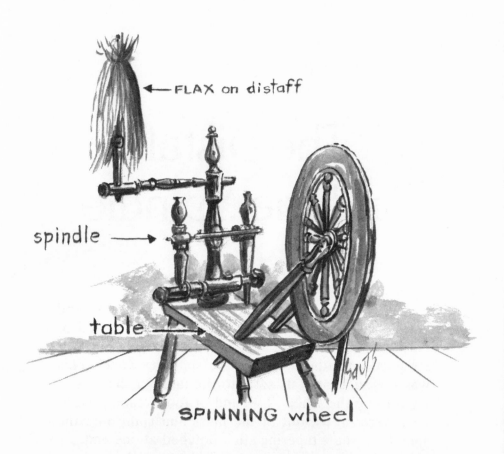

← FLAX on distaff

spindle →

table →

SPINNING wheel

spindle held in the other hand. They did their spinning while occupied with other chores or while walking in the garden.

The Greek islands showed their respect for women's crafts by naming the great warrior goddess, Pallas Athene, the patron of spinning and weaving. Greek mythology also relates that the wondrous Helen of Troy was given a golden distaff. Poets were known to make gifts of ivory distaffs.

All over the great Eastern empires into the newly formed nation-states of Europe, women were the spinners. They made the cotton, flax, and woolen yarn that became the cloth for the dazzling costumes worn by kings and queens. Among ordinary people each family did its own spinning.

Only silk had a different producer. In Asia and Africa where the silkworm flourished, people learned to unwind the long delicate threads of silk that made up the cocoon.

Not until the fourteenth or fifteenth centuries did the nature of spinning change from a handcraft to a technological device. The spinning wheel put together the distaff and spindle into one mechanism. Though spinning at the wheel demanded as much time as hand spinning, women were able to produce more yarn.

In the cargo that came with colonial settlers, the Western world sent the spinning wheel over to the homeland of the Indian people. Mary Allen and others introduced the spinning wheel into the New England woodlands.

"Tomorrow Dances Behind the Sun..."

Yawata, the basket maker, and Mary Allen, the spinner, never met, though each knew about the other. In many ways it was a pity, for Yawata could have passed on to Mary valuable information about the riches and dangers of the woodlands. Mary could have given Yawata and her people the option of absorbing what they wanted from another way of life.

These two had so much in common. They were hardworking women, parents, and homemakers. Each was artistic and creative, the backbone of home and community.

But more drew them apart than pulled them together. They saw things differently. Their vision was formed by different experiences and needs.

Yawata felt she was part of the land she lived on with its abundant woods, flowers, and animals. The sky overhead and the brooks rippling through the woodlands were sources of joy. The very earth was vital to her life and her culture.

Mary, looking over the farmland, also loved it for its

abundant harvest, its flowers and trees. She loved the land not only for its beauty but because it belonged to her. It was hers. Her colonial neighbors enjoyed the same feeling of private ownership: the land and its fruits and berries were theirs. Fences marked off their fields from others.

Not only did Yawata and Mary have different ways of looking at things, but Mary arrived with the conviction that Europeans were superior to the native people, that she and Yawata were in no way equal. Such thinking made it easy for the colonists to push the native people around, to take over their land, and enforce European ideas by freely using their superior weapons, muskets, and rifles. The first years of trying to be friends gave way to violence.

Yawata and most of her people were wiped out. At first disease took its toll. Then came wars and murder. Yawata's descendants no longer made baskets in the same way.

Her people used cloth for clothing, metal pots for the household, blankets for warmth. Indian survivors of wars were often forced to become slaves. At one point colonial leaders put Indian women into a school to teach them spinning in order to relieve colonists of this tedious work.

Throughout the country so many Indians were killed that they were called the Vanishing Americans. But they did not vanish. Survivors held on to their long, arduous history and culture. They tenaciously regarded the earth as theirs. They struggled and demanded their rights. Today there are Indian scholars, writers, painters, and sculptors portraying their side of history, telling of their immense suffering.

There are also Indian women basket makers (joined

53

by a few Indian men) who work with their hands in the traditional way. Many are noted for the rare beauty of their work, and they can be found wherever Indians have settled, in the Northeast, the Northwest, or the Southwest.

Gracing the wide field of crafts are spinners. They enjoy the rhythm of the wheel and the feel of delicate yarn that will be made into rare pieces of cloth.

Today the basket maker and the spinner respect each other's craft and talent and each other's right to enjoy a different cultural heritage. They also recognize how much they have in common as women.

The Native American poet Peter Blue Cloud says it this way:

TOMORROW

We have wept the blood
                    of countless ages
as each of us raised high
                    the lance of hate. . . .
Now let us dry our tears
                    and learn the dance
and chant of the life cycle
tomorrow dances behind the sun
                    in sacred promise
of things to come for children
                    not yet born,
for ours is the potential of truly
                    lasting beauty
born of hope and shaped by deed.
Now let us lay the lance of hate
                    upon this soil.

Appendix

THE WAMPANOAG CALENDAR

The Months	*The Moons*
(1) January, February	Squocheekeeswush, when the sun has the strength to thaw
(2) February, March	Wapicummilcum, when ice in the river is gone
(3) March, April	Namassack Keeswuch, the time of catching fish
(4) Late April, Early May	Sequanankeeswush, when they set corn
(5) May, June	Moonesquanimock, when the women weed corn
(6) June, July	Towwakeeswosh, when they hill the corn

(7) July to late August   Matterllawawkeeswush, squash ripe, beans edible

(8) August, September   Neepunna Keeswosh, corn is edible; or Micheennee Keeswosh, everlasting flies

(9) September, October   Pohquitaqunk Keeswush, the "middle between" or Hawkswawney Taquontikeeswush, the harvest moon

(10) October, November   Pepewarr, white frost

(11) November, December   Quinne Keeswush, the long moon

(12) December, January   Papsaquoho, to about January 6; Lowatanassick, mid-winter; Paponakeeswush, winter month

Suggested Reading

Earle, A.M. *Child-Life in Colonial Days.* Darby, Pennsylvania: Arden Library, 1978.

Glubok, Shirley. *The Art of the Woodland Indians.* New York: Macmillan Publishing Co., Inc., 1976.

Handbook of the North American Indian, William C. Sturtevant, Gen. Ed. Vol. 15, Washington: Smithsonian Institution, 1978.

Lasky, Kathryn. *The Weaver's Gift.* New York: Frederick Warne, 1980.

Parker, Arthur C. *The Indian How Book.* New York: Dover, 1975.

Siegel, Beatrice. *A New Look at the Pilgrims, Why They Came to America.* New York: Walker and Co., 1977.

Warren, Ruth. *A Pictorial History of Women in America.* New York: Crown Publishers, Inc., 1975.

Welch, Martha McKeen. *Sunflower.* New York: Dodd Mead and Co., 1980.

Wilbur, C. Keith. *The New England Indians.* Connecticut: Globe Pequot Press, 1978.

NOTES

This book was written with the cooperation of many people but I would like to thank in particular Mary Davis, Librarian, the Museum of the American Indian Library in New York City, New York; and Ann McMullen, Curator, American Indian Archaeological Institute, Inc., in Washington, Connecticut.

The Wampanoag Indian Calendar is reprinted with the permission of Dr. Milton A. Travers, author of the book, *One of the Keys: The Wampanoag Indian Contribution 1676-1776-1976,* Dartmouth, Mass., 1975.

The poem, "Tomorrow", is reprinted with the permission of the author, Aroniawenrate/Peter Blue Cloud.

"Atisket atasket" is an old American nursery song that was titled *I Sent A Letter to My Love* when it appeared in 1879 in a book by A.H. Rosewig, *Nursery Songs and Games.*

Index

Achenes. *See* sunflower seeds

Animals, 14, 18, 20, 23, 31, 32–33, 51
  domesticated, 39

Artichokes, 18

Athene, Pallas, 48

Autumn, 10, 18, 32

Awls, 23, 24

Baby carrier, 21, 32

Babylonia, 47

Baskets
  as artistic expression, 23, 24, 27
  backpack, 19, 21
  as communal activity, 23–24
  cornhusk, 19
  corn washing, 19
  designs of, 23, 27, 28
  fish, 19
  handle, 19, 20
  history of, 21
  and Indians, 10, 15, 21–27, 29, 31, 51, 52, 54
  learning how to make, 23, 24
  lid, 19
  makers, 15, 20, 21, 29, 31, 51, 52, 54, 55
  and modern technology, 9–10
  tools for weaving, 23
  weaving materials, 20–23, 25, 26, 27, 31

weaving methods,
25–26, 27
use of, 20, 21, 23
Beads, 23
Beans, 18
Berries, 20, 21, 23, 31,
52
Birds, 11, 18, 23, 31
Blue Cloud, Peter, 54
Bread, 20, 32
Buckets, 32
Butter, churning of, 38

Candles, 38
Carding, 44, 45
Cattails, 20
Chisels, 15, 29
Cloth, weaving of, 47.
See also spinning
wheel
Clothes, 41
Coiling, 27
Colonists, 10, 31,
33–36, 39–40, 52.
See also Europe
Corn, 18, 20, 32
husks, 31
planting of, 35

Devil's Claw, 22
Diseases, 33–34, 52

Distaff, 47, 49
as symbol, 47
Dyes, 23, 31, 32

Egypt, 47
England, 37
Europe. *See also* colo-
nists
technology of, 10
women of, 48–49

Family, 15, 41–42, 44
Feathers, 23, 27
Fences, 52
Fish, 20
Flax
-breaker, 43
fiber, 43, 47, 49
stems, 43
seeds, 43
Flowers, 23, 51, 52. *See
also* sunflowers
Food, 15, 18, 20, 31, 39.
See also sunflower
seeds

Gookin, Daniel, 31
Graphite, 31
Grass, 20, 21, 22, 26,
27, 31
Greece, 47, 48